A New Home for a Pirate

RONDA ARMITAGE ☠ HOLLY SWAIN

PUFFIN

Jed was a pirate
      but he didn't enjoy it.
It was a tight squeeze on the ship
and it was always bobbing about.

Every day
Jed was seasick.
Every night Jed dreamt
of a house
that stood still.

One morning,
Jed announced he was leaving.

"I
want
a house
that stands still
with a view from a hill
and a roof that's blue like the sky.

And when I've found it
you can all come to stay."

"Splice the mainbrace!"
   exclaimed his mum and dad.
They'd never had a landlubber
   in the family.
      But they could see he'd
made up his mind and they
   liked the bit about visiting.

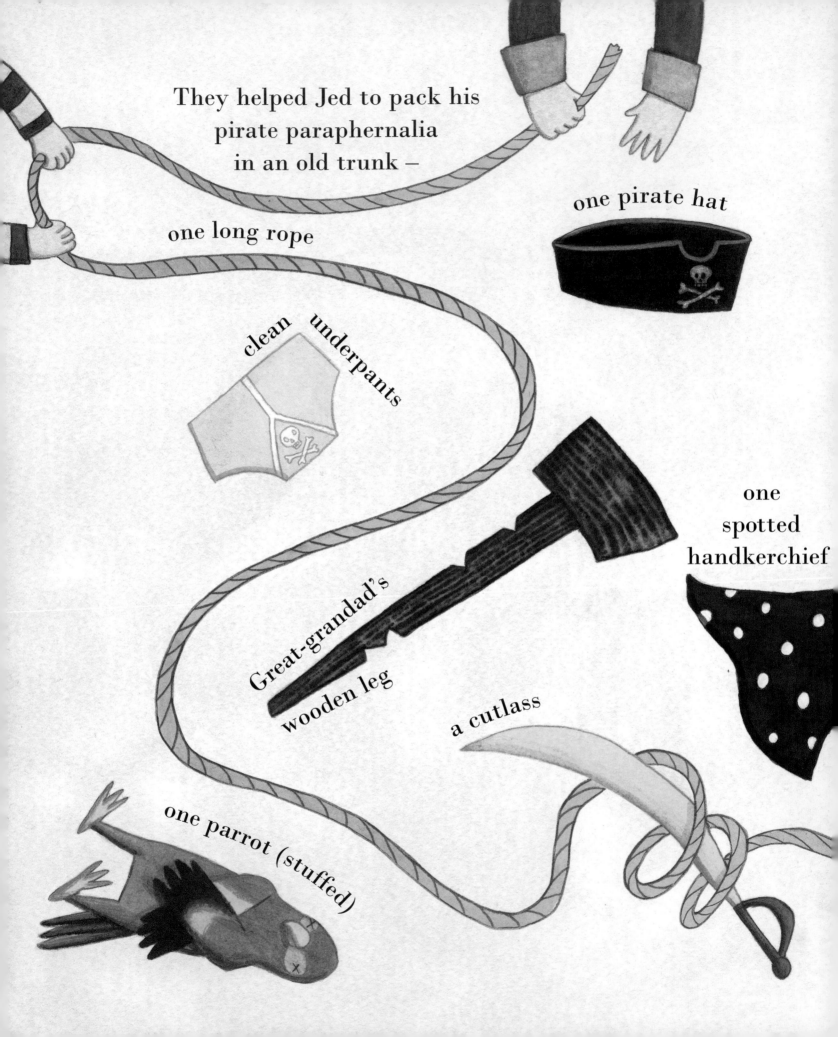

They helped Jed to pack his
pirate paraphernalia
in an old trunk –

one long rope

one pirate hat

clean underpants

one spotted handkerchief

Great-grandad's wooden leg

a cutlass

one parrot (stuffed)

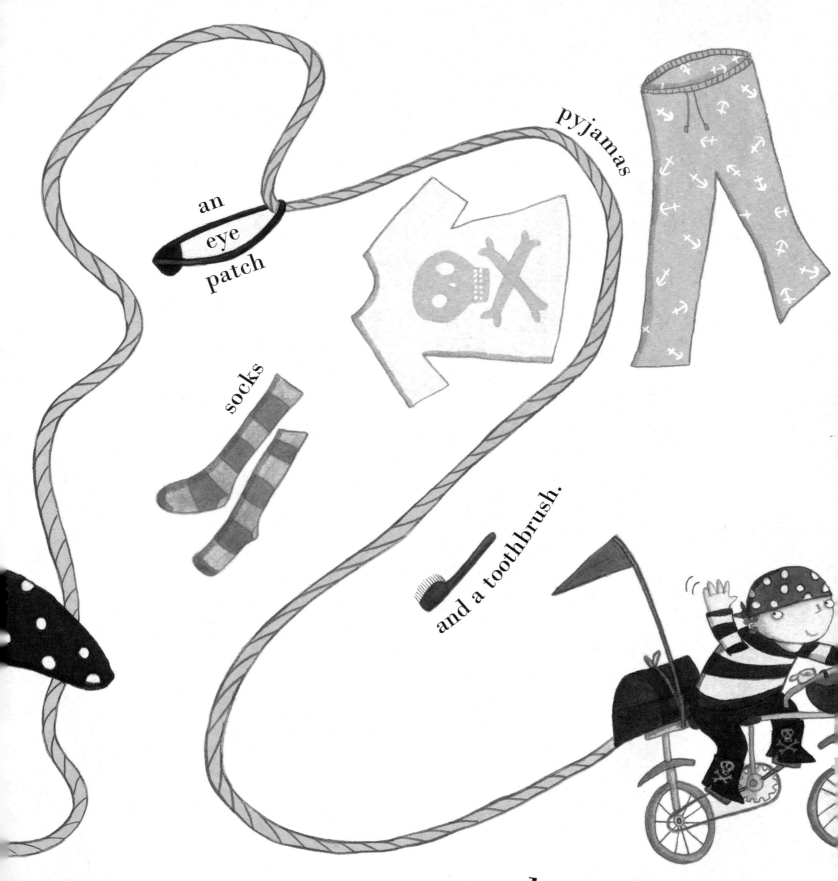

pyjamas

an
eye
patch

socks

and a toothbrush.

"Cheeriyo-ho-ho,"
called Jed as he cycled away.

He came to a forest.
A bird was squawking.
"Please can you help?
My nest is a mess."

Jed scratched his head.
"Shiver Me Timbers!" he exclaimed.
"I've got the very thing."

He took out his pirate hat.
The nest fitted perfectly.

"Thank you," said Bird.
"You're very kind for a pirate."

"I'm not a pirate any more,"
explained Jed.
"I'm looking for a new home."

"I
want
a house
that stands still,
with a view from a hill
and a roof that's blue like the sky."

"Will there be a tree?"
asked Bird.
"Of course," said Jed.
"Come with me.
We'll look for a new
home together."

They came to a field.
A sheep was ba^aa^aing loudly.
"Please can you help?
I'm all tangled in brambles."

Jed scratched his head.

"Shiver me timbers!"
he exclaimed.
"I've got the very thing."

He took out his cutlass and sliced the sheep free.
"Oh, thank you," she said.
"You're very kind for a pirate."

"I'm not a pirate any more," explained Jed.
"I'm looking for a new home."

"I
want
a house
that stands still,
with a view from a hill
and a roof that's blue like the sky.
With a stretching-high tree."

"Will there be a grassy field?"
asked Sheep.
"Of course," said Jed.
"Come with us.
We'll look for a new
home together."

They came to a high bank.
An old dog lay whimpering.
"Please can you help? I've broken my leg."

Jed scratched his head.

"Shiver me timbers!" he exclaimed.
"I've got the very thing."

whimper
whimper

Jed took out his great-grandad's wooden leg
and tied it on with the spotted handkerchief.

"Oh, thank you," said Old Dog.
"You're very kind for a pirate."

"I'm not a pirate any more," explained Jed.
"I'm looking for a new home."

"I
want
a house
that stands still,
with a view from a hill
and a roof that's blue like the sky.
With a stretching-high tree
in a field (bramble-free)."

"Will there be a doormat?"
asked Old Dog.
"Of course," said Jed.
"Come with us.
We'll look for a new
home together."

They came
to an open gate.
A red bull was tossing his horns.
"I want to chase you," he roared.

Jed scratched his head.

"Shiver me timbers!" he exclaimed.
"Luckily, I've got the very thing."

Jed took out the rope and
hauled the bike
into a tree.

HELP
HELP

MOO!

Farmer Ted
came running.

"Shoo, shoo!" he shouted
and chased Red Bull
back into the field.

"Thank you," said Jed.
"You're very kind for a farmer."

But Farmer Ted sighed.
"I'm not really a farmer any more.
There's only Red Bull and me.
I'd rather be a pirate.
Yes, that's the life for me.
On a rollicking, rolling ship,
on a rollicking, rolling sea."

"We
want
a house
that stands still,
with a view from a hill
and a roof that's blue like the sky.
With a stretching-high tree
in a field (bramble-free)
and a doormat where
Old Dog can lie."

"Come with me,"
said Farmer Ted.
"I think I've got the
very thing."

Jed sighed. "I'm not
really a pirate any more,
my friends and I are looking
for a new home, too."

"A house like mine?" asked Ted.
"Perfect," replied Jed.

"A ship like mine?" asked Jed.
"Wonderful," replied Ted.

"Let's swap!" they said together.

- Pirate talk
- Reading a treasure map
- Gangplank walking
- Cutlass class

SEA

SHARKS

Jed introduced Ted to his family. "Ted wants to be a pirate," he explained. "Can you help?"

"Oo-aar-r-gh!" they shouted. "We'll show 'im. We're the best pirate teachers in the world."

Oo-aar-r-gh, me hearties, you bilge-wallowing buccaneers.

Ted passed all the pirate tests. The pirates were so impressed they invited him to join their mucky crew immediately.

Ted liked his new home.
"Oo-aar-r-gh!
This is the life for me.
On a rollicking, rolling ship,
on a rollicking, rolling sea.

Cheeriyo-ho-ho,
me hearties."

And Jed knew he would be a
very wicked pirate indeed.

Jed liked his new home, too.
Bird sang in the tree.
Sheep munched in the field.
And Old Dog slept on
the doormat.

tweet tweet

"I've
a house
that stands still,
with a view from a hill
and a roof that's
blue like the sky.

A perfect new home
for a pirate."

mool

baaa!

The End
And if you look closely, you'll see what happened
to that eyepatch and parrot (stuffed).

To Tomas – R. A.

For my sister and brother,

with love x – H. S.

PUFFIN BOOKS
Published by the Penguin Group: London, New York, Australia, Canada, India, Ireland, New Zealand and South Africa
Penguin Books Ltd, Registered Offices: 80 Strand, London WC2R 0RL, England
puffinbooks.com   001 – 10 9 8 7 6 5 4 3 2 1
First published 2007   Published in this edition 2011   Text copyright © Ronda Armitage, 2007   Illustrations copyright © Holly Swain, 2007